This
Harry and
the
Dinosaurs
book belongs to

. . . . . . . . . . . . . . . . . . . . . . .

SCELIDOSAURUS
(ske-LI-doh-SAW-rus)

TYRANNOSAURUS
(tie-RAN-oh-SAW-rus)

TRICERATOPS
(try-SER-a-tops)

KANGAROO
(KAN-gah-roo)

STEGOSAURUS
(STEG-oh-SAW-rus)

PTERODACTYL
(TER-oh-DAC-til)

APATOSAURUS
(a-PAT-oh-SAW-rus)

ANCHISAURUS
(AN-ki-SAW-rus)

*For those inspirational and life-enhancing Aussies – my baby sister*
*Ellie Harvey and her two little darlings, Tom and Alice – with love.*
*And for Gordon Jackson, the founder of Koala Books, who believed*
*in Harry and the Bucketful of Dinosaurs from the beginning – with gratitude. – I. W.*


*To Wendy – A. R.*

PUFFIN BOOKS

UK | USA | Canada | Ireland | Australia
India | New Zealand | South Africa

Puffin Books is part of the Penguin Random House group of companies
whose addresses can be found at global.penguinrandomhouse.com.

www.penguin.co.uk   www.puffin.co.uk   www.ladybird.co.uk

 Penguin
Random House
UK

First published 2012
This edition published 2016
004

Text copyright © Ian Whybrow, 2012
Illustrations copyright © Adrian Reynolds, 2012
All rights reserved
The moral right of the author and illustrator has been asserted

Made and printed in China

ISBN: 978-0-141-37507-6

All correspondence to:
Puffin Books
Penguin Random House Children's
80 Strand, London WC2R 0RL

# Harry and the Dinosaurs go on Holiday

Ian Whybrow  Adrian Reynolds

PUFFIN

Harry was showing the dinosaurs his postcard from Auntie Ellie in Australia.

"Look!" he said. "Tomorrow we're all going to Australia for our holiday. I can't wait, but I wish you could come too, Nan."

Nan said, "Never mind about me. Can you see Sydney, right round the other side of the world!"

Pterodactyl said, "I'll come, Harry! Flying is easy-peasy."
Tyrannosaurus said, "Raaah! I don't like flying!
Can we swim instead?"
But Harry said no, that would be much too slow.

Next day they went to the airport.
The dinosaurs were a bit nervous about flying and going such a long way from home, but Nan soon cheered them up. She gave them a special present to open when they arrived.

What a lot of people!
And what a long way for Harry to pull his dino-case! Everybody loved going on the escalator.
"Raaah!" the dinosaurs said. "This is just like riding on a diplodocus's neck!"

After take-off, Harry showed the dinosaurs some
of the animals they might see. Tyrannosaurus loved
the great white shark.
"Sharp teeth! Like mine," he said. "RAAAH!"
And Stegosaurus liked the kangaroo. "He's like me!" he
said. "We can both whack things with our tails. Swish!"

Anchisaurus said, "I would like to be in a picture with a duck-billed platypus because we've both got strange and interesting feet."
Sam said they were all stupid because dinosaurs are nothing like Australian animals.
That was why her earphones got hooked out.

POP!

OUCH!

When they landed, Harry showed the customs officer
the dinosaurs' passports.
The man said, "I will let them into the country if you
can tell me all their names."
So Harry told him and he didn't make one single mistake.
"Welcome to Australia!" said the officer.

Anchi saurus
Stego saurus
Tyranno saurus
Pterodactyl
Scelido saurus
Triceratops
Apato saurus

Auntie Ellie was waiting at the barrier
with Harry's cousins, Alice and Tom.

"Hello!" she said. "Hats on, everyone!
It's hot outside!"

That night, after everyone had settled in,
there was a barbie in the garden.

There were possums in the gum trees and Harry
helped Tom grill the prawns with dipping sauce.
They were nice, but some people were too tired
to eat because of jetlag!

The next day the dinosaurs were grumpy
and wouldn't behave.
"RAAAH! We want Nan!" they grumbled.
"We don't want to go to the beach!"

Harry wouldn't get dressed and then he made a fuss about
the suncream. Mum could see that everyone was tired
and a little bit homesick. "I've got an idea," she said.
"This is just the moment to open Nan's present."

"Wow! A camera!" said Alice.
"Nice one, mate! Now you can show
Nan what we're all up to!"

They did lots of brilliant Australian things on that holiday.
Each day was a new adventure. There were plenty of fantastic
places to explore and lots of new things to eat.

Harry and the dinosaurs really enjoyed playing
at the beach and watching the surfers.
Then they built a mega sandosaurus with their
buckets and spades.
The lifeguards loved it and showed everyone
how to do posing for the camera.

"RAAAH!" said Tyrannosaurus.
"Look at us posing too! Cheese!"

Every day was full of fun.

And every evening, before they went to bed,
Mum helped them send photos home to Nan
so that she could join in too.

But what Harry and the dinosaurs liked best –
especially Anchisaurus – was the day Auntie Ellie
took them to the wildlife sanctuary.

At last! Anchisaurus could be in a picture
with a duck-billed platypus.
"Three raaahs for the platypus!"
cheered the dinosaurs.

When the time came to go home, everyone felt sad.
"Never mind," said Harry. "Let's pack lots of things to
remind us of all the fun we had on holiday."

On the plane, the dinosaurs said, "Raaahh!
We all like flying now and we like Australia!"
"Yes, but home's nice too," said Harry, "and we'll
be able to tell Nan all about our adventures."

Nan and Mr Oakley were waiting when they landed.

ARRIVALS

"Thank you for sending all them lovely photos, my dear!"
said Nan. "They made me feel I was right there with you."
"And thank you for your special present!" said Harry.
"Now we can always remember our wonderful holiday!"

"And lifeguard-posing!"
said the dinosaurs. "RAAAAH!"
ENDOSAURUS

SCELIDOSAURUS
(ske-LI-doh-SAW-rus)

TYRANNOSAURUS
(tie-RAN-oh-SAW-rus)

TRICERATOPS
(try-SER-a-tops)

KANGAROO
(KAN-gah-roo)

STEGOSAURUS
(STEG-oh-SAW-rus)

PTERODACTYL
(TER-oh-DAC-til)

APATOSAURUS
(a-PAT-oh-SAW-rus)

ANCHISAURUS
(AN-ki-SAW-rus)

SCELIDOSAURUS
(ske-LI-doh-SAW-rus)

TYRANNOSAURUS
(tie-RAN-oh-SAW-rus)

KANGAROO
(KAN-gah-roo)

TRICERATOPS
(try-SER-a-tops)

STEGOSAURUS
(STEG-oh-SAW-rus)

PTERODACTYL
(TER-oh-DAC-til)

APATOSAURUS
(a-PAT-oh-SAW-rus)

ANCHISAURUS
(AN-ki-SAW-rus)